CN00864362

STINKERBELL

J.J. MURHALL

BLOOMSBURY

This book is dedicated especially to
Michael and Saoirse Ruby
And to all little stinkers everywhere,
young and old, who know how to
"Wake up and dream"

(with special thanks to Paul Lloyd)

First published in Great Britain in 1996
Text copyright © 1996 J.J. Murhall
Illustrations © 1996 Tony Blundell
The moral right of the author has been asserted

Bloomsbury Publishing PLC, 38 Soho Square, London W1D 3HB
A CIP catalogue record for this book is available from The British Library
ISBN 0 7475 2511 0 pb
ISBN 0 7475 2510 2 hb

10 9 8 7 6 5 4 3 2 1

All papers used by Bloomsbury Publishing are natural, recyclable
products made from wood grown in well-managed forests.
The manufacturing processes conform to the
environmental regulations of the country of origin.

Text design by AB3
Cover design by Alison Withey
Printed and bound in Great Britain by Clays Ltd, St Ives plc

CHAPTER
ONE

EVERYONE'S HEARD of good fairies, of bad fairies, of elves, pixies, goblins and gnomes. Everybody knows that they live at the bottom of the garden, or in the middle of a wood, most probably under a toadstool. However, modern fairies have had to move with the times, and in towns and cities all over the world they

now make their homes in the most unusual places. In fact, you can find them almost anywhere just as long as there is a bit of greenery – you may even find one in the window box of a tower block! The fairies at number 11 Azalea Avenue are lucky. They live down at the bottom of a huge garden. Between the shrubs, under the shed and inside the greenhouse there exists a world not unlike your own, where fairies sleep, and work and go to school. It's a place where they play, make friends, and sometimes fall out with each other.

Now, most fairies are generally well behaved, and they may well go on to pass their exams and become tooth fairies. But some are not. Some can be quite naughty. The more adventurous and reckless fairies might well ring on your door bell and run away, or shove your dad's car keys down the back of the settee. On a particularly daring day, they may even ring up your mum while she's in the bath, and then, while she's dripping soapsuds on the hall carpet, and trying to stop the towel from showing her bottom, they pretend it's a wrong number.

Fairly naughty stuff, I'm sure you'll agree. But this kind of behaviour is all very tame compared to the antics of one particular fairy. *She* would turn her nose up at such trivial tricks. For this little minx is very haughty and incredibly naughty. She is bad and she is glad. She's dinky, stinky and downright cheeky. And her name is – STINKERBELL!

Quite how Stinkerbell came to arrive at number 11

Azalea Avenue is a bit of a mystery. She was found one day by some other fairies, floating on a rose petal in the birdbath in the middle of the garden. She was very grubby, with a button nose smudged all over with dirt, and a chipped front tooth. She sat crossed-legged and was dressed in a tiny jaded silver jacket that was far too small, matching torn tights, and a little skirt rather like a tutu, only it was made out of little slivers of potato peelings. Attached to her big toe was a note which read:

PLEASE COULD YOU LOOK AFTER OUR DAUGHTER.
HER NAME IS STINKERBELL.
WE HAVE HAD TO LEAVE HER
BECAUSE

Unfortunately the rest of the message had been chewed off and eaten by Stinkerbell who had been feeling a bit bored and peckish. When asked about her parents' whereabouts, Stinkerbell said she couldn't remember anything about them. All she could remember was falling into a deep sleep, and then waking up, much to her disgust, in the birdbath.

Wrinkling her nose in distaste she said, "I got the shock of my life when I woke up surrounded by all this water, I can tell you. I've *never* taken a bath before and I'm six now. I know I'm six because I've got six teeth, well, five and a half if you count my chipped one – look." And she opened her mouth really wide and thrust it towards the two fairies who had found her.

"Yes, very nice, dear," said the older fairy, Mrs Gildalily. "Now let's get you down."

And the two fairies flew down with Stinkerbell between them, onto the lawn below.

"I can't wait to learn to fly properly," said Stinkerbell, skipping ahead. "I want my own wand as well, and I want to be a princess. I want to be the dirtiest princess in the neighbourhood."

She turned and looked at the two elderly fairies. "Do you think I could be one? Are there any princesses in this garden?"

"There are no princesses, but there is a king and queen," replied Mrs Gildalily. "And they have just had a brand-new baby boy."

Stinkerbell didn't look too impressed, and went skipping off again with her little plaits bouncing up and down.

"She's so sweet," said Mrs Gildalily to her friend Mrs Clump, who was a very wise old tooth fairy.

"Adorable," replied Mrs Clump. "Filthy. But quite adorable." And they both hurried off after her.

It was true. Stinkerbell did look the picture of innocence. But appearances can be deceiving, and it soon became clear that life at number 11 Azalea Avenue would *never* be quite the same again.

Stinkerbell was hiding. She was hiding from next-door's cat. He'd already chased her up the garden path, through the sandpit and twice around the fishpond. For some reason he seemed to be very attracted to Stinkerbell – probably because wherever she went, a strange smell went too.

Anyway, she was now crouched in the lap of one of the plastic gnomes that stood by the fish pond. These two creatures were known as "The Great Grinning Ones", and were the most feared things in the garden. Even the King was scared of them. Nobody knew how they had got there, or why they never, ever seemed to move. Not even blink. But everyone believed that they moved around at night and spied on them by peeping through their letter-boxes, and peering down their chimneys when they were asleep.

Stinkerbell couldn't understand what all the fuss was about. She thought they were very comfortable to sit on, and apart from that, this was the second time they'd saved her from the jaws of that monstrous beast from next door.

She peered over The Great Grinning Ones' knees to

see whether the coast was clear. The cat seemed to have vanished, and the garden, apart from a few fairies going about some chores, seemed remarkably quiet.

Suddenly, Stinkerbell spotted something lying in the sandpit. From a distance it looked like a tiny person, not much taller than Stinkerbell, only dressed in the strangest of clothes. Stinkerbell went over to investigate.

It was a doll, an Action Man doll, dressed in combat gear and big black boots.

"Hello," said Stinkerbell, dragging him upright and leaning him against a sand mound. "Are you OK? Or were you just having a snooze? I sometimes like to have a snooze at this time of the day."

The doll stared dumbly back at her.

"You're not very talkative, are you?" continued Stinkerbell, dusting him down. "And what a horrible shade of green you're wearing."

Stinkerbell peered closely at him. "Oo. How did you get that little scar on the side of your face? Was it that cat? Because it's nearly had me a few times."

Stinkerbell sat back and sighed. She thought maybe he was suffering from battle fatigue. Whatever it was, he was certainly pretty boring. However, his boots had caught her eye. They were big and black and shiny. Stinkerbell thought they were the best boots she had ever seen. First, she stared down at her own filthy little bare feet, and then she glanced over her shoulder to make sure there was no one around. Then very care-

fully, so as not to disturb him, she pulled off one boot and then the other, and as quick as a flash she put them on. They looked enormous, big and clompy on her tiny legs, but Stinkerbell was thrilled.

"I hope you don't mind," she said, smiling at the doll. "But you don't look like you're going anywhere, and I think they look far better on me, don't you?" And she turned around and stomped out of the sandpit like a fairy elephant, in search of someone she could show them off to.

At the entrance to the bottom of the garden was a long garden seat. This was guarded by two pixie sentries who stood at either end, straight-backed, with their wands down by their sides.

"Halt. Who goes there?" said one of the pixies as Stinkerbell approached.

"You know who it is, you old silly," replied

Stinkerbell. "It's me, Stinkerbell. Do you like my new boots? Aren't they just the *best* boots you've ever clapped eyes on?"

The pixie eyed her suspiciously. He was very wary of this grubby little fairy who had just moved in, and he had his reasons. For the very day she'd arrived at the bottom of the garden he had been on duty. Stinkerbell had begged him to let her take a look at his wand. It was a particularly nice gold one, with a very ornate, carved handle. When it became clear that Stinkerbell was *not* going to leave unless she got what she wanted, he'd relented and had handed it over to her.

"Only for a moment, though," he whispered under his breath. "If the King sees you, there'll be trouble."

Stinkerbell had ignored him. This was the very first time that she had ever held a wand, and it felt fantastic. There was a tingling sensation that started at her fingertips, and then seemed to dance all the way up her arm. Stinkerbell had then begun to wave it wildly in the air as she danced about.

Then suddenly she'd tripped over a stone, and PING! the end of the wand had touched the pixie's shoulder.

In an instant, he turned into half a frog. Luckily, the other pixie on duty at the time had very quickly changed him back. But still, even after three days, he seemed to be suffering from the after-effects, because every so often when he was supposed to be keeping very still, he'd break into a hop. As he let Stinkerbell

go through today, she could have sworn she heard him croak as well!

The King was standing over by the barbecue, which was his winter palace. He was overseeing his annual move.

Every year, at the start of the summer, he and his family would vacate it and take up residence in the enormous eaves of the garden umbrella. And then, as the chillier nights set in, and when the barbecue had cooled down, they moved back in again. Though the interior ALWAYS had to be redecorated as every year it ended up completely black and covered in grease.

"Hello, your Majesty," said Stinkerbell with a smile. "Do you need a hand?"

"No, thank you," replied the King. "I have my helpers. In fact, I'd like you to meet Douglas. This little fellow is probably the most helpful and tidy young pixie in the garden."

Stinkerbell looked over at Douglas. He was very small, and pale, with a round face, and he was wearing extremely thick round glasses, through which he blinked nervously at Stinkerbell. He wore a woolly hat, and attached to the end of it was a tiny silver bell that jingled every time he moved his head.

"Yes," continued the King, "we're very proud of Douglas. He's a very ambitious boy. He starts Charm School tomorrow, and he's *very* determined to pass his exams, get his proper wings, and of course his wand." The King patted Douglas on the top of his head. The tiny bell rang, and Douglas looked up at the King adoringly.

"Tell Stinkerbell what your ambition is, Douglas," said the King.

"Yes, what do you want to be?" asked Stinkerbell eagerly. "I want to be a princess. I want to be the dirtiest, filthiest princess in the street."

Douglas sniffed distastefully. "My ambition is to be in charge of the compost heap over in the corner of the garden," he declared proudly. "I'm going to work my way up and up until the job's mine."

Stinkerbell was not impressed. Being in charge of a compost heap sounded to her like a very dull job indeed. In fact, she thought Douglas was quite the

dullest pixie she'd ever met, and apart from that, he was *much* too clean.

"Well, I must be off to check that everything has been put into the new palace," said the King with a smile. "Now, I hope that you two will become friends. Stinkerbell, I think you could learn a few tricks about good behaviour and cleanliness from Douglas, you know." And off he went towards the garden umbrella.

Stinkerbell and Douglas eyed each other suspiciously. Then Stinkerbell spotted a large sack amongst the King's pots and pans and bed linen that was waiting to be moved. Printed on the side of it in bold lettering were the words:

AA NYMPH LTD
HIGH QUALITY
FAIRY DUST
50grms

"*I'll* show you a trick if you want," said Stinkerbell, striding over to the sack and opening it. She then proceeded to tip the whole sack under the wheels of the barbecue.

Douglas bounced up and down, his bell ringing frantically.

"What are you doing, Stinkerbell?" he hissed. "That's the King's personal fairy dust! You'll get into the most terrible trouble." And he bounced up and down even harder.

"Oh don't be such a sourpuss," replied Stinkerbell. "It's only a bit of fun." And she picked up one of the King's ceremonial wands and waved it around.

Suddenly, there was the most tremendous whizzing and banging noise, like an enormous firework going off, and the King's barbecue palace shot straight up into the air like a rocket!

Stinkerbell and Douglas looked up into the bright blue sky as the huge, round object went hurtling across it at incredible speed. It seemed to go on forever, and the other fairies who were scattered about stopped what they were doing and watched it in utter amazement. Then it flew right over the King's head. The King looked up, aghast. Then finally the winter palace made its descent, and catapulted straight over next-door's fence, where it landed upside down, slap-bang in the middle of the newly-mown lawn with its wheels spinning furiously.

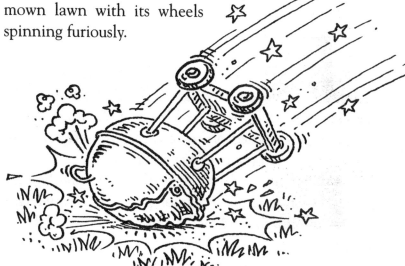

"Oh dear. Oh deary, deary me," said Stinkerbell, surveying the carnage through a crack in the fence. "That was some powerful stuff." And she chewed her lip nervously as she saw the King striding towards her, his face crimson with rage.

"Stinkerbell!" he roared. "What have you done?"

Stinkerbell bowed her head. "I only wanted to move it a few feet," she said sheepishly. "I just wanted to show Douglas what I could do."

Meanwhile, Douglas's bottom lip had begun to quiver, and then his little bell started as well, and he looked like he was about to burst into tears.

The King shook his head. "I think the best place for you, my girl, is Charm School," he said. "You may be a little too young, but it's high time you learnt to behave yourself properly. So you can start tomorrow along with all the other pupils."

A little smile started to light up Stinkerbell's sorry face.

"But put one boot out of place, Stinkerbell," continued the King gravely, "and I'll banish you from the garden. I mean it. Now. Let this be a warning to you."

And he marched off to organise the safe return of the crashed and mangled barbecue.

Stinkerbell could hardly believe her ears. *She* was going to start Charm School. And that could only mean one thing. And *that thing* was LONG and THIN and SPARKLY and quite, quite beautiful. Yes, she was going to get her very own wand.

The next morning all the other fairies were washed and scrubbed and seated at their desks eager to learn. But

Stinkerbell was as scruffy as ever and now even her desk was a mess. It was already strewn with bits of paper, an old half-chewed cardboard carton, and an apple core that she was saving for later. The inside of her desk was even worse. It was jammed full of old comics and bags that she'd picked up on the way. In fact, it was so full she was having trouble shutting the lid.

However, Stinkerbell was very keen indeed to learn to fly well and acquire her wand, so when the teacher came in, she sat up straight, stuck her gum behind her ear for safe-keeping and listened attentively.

"Good morning, everyone," said the teacher. "My name is Miss Primslip. Now, who can tell me what the school motto of the three M's stands for?"

All the little fairy hands shot up, including Stinkerbell's. Stinkerbell was so keen to be noticed, she proceeded to stand on top of her desk.

Miss Primslip pointed at Stinkerbell. "Yes, you. The, er, grubby one. What's your name? And you can sit back down now."

"My name's Stinkerbell, Miss Dimwit," replied Stinkerbell climbing off the table. "And the three M's of the Charm School stand for . . ." Here Stinkerbell took a deep breath and announced proudly:

"Make More Mess!"

Well, there was a gasp all around the classroom and a few stifled giggles.

Miss Primslip looked very taken aback. "It most certainly does not mean that," she replied curtly, "and don't call me Dimwit, my name's Primslip, you rude little girl!"

"I'm ever so sorry, Miss Bigtwit," replied Stinkerbell, "only I must have misheard. I think I must have stuck my gum *in* my ear instead of behind it."

Meanwhile, Douglas, who was sitting right in front of Stinkerbell, had been bouncing up and down in his seat, the little bell on top of his hat frantically ringing. He could hardly contain himself.

"Yes, the little pixie with the glasses. What's your name? And what's the answer?"

"My name's Douglas, Miss, and the motto stands for 'Manners Mean Most'." He looked very pleased with himself.

"Well done, Douglas. 'Make More Mess', indeed, a fairy should never, *ever* be untidy."

At this point Stinkerbell could feel all eyes turn slowly towards her, and suddenly she felt very grubby and very scruffy. However, she sat back in her chair and with a grin and a shrug of her shoulders she announced matter-of-factly: "I don't like baths. They make me go all crinkly."

From then on, Stinkerbell's first day at Charm School went from bad to worse – *much* worse. For it was after lunch that Stinkerbell did the most terrible, dreadful thing.

All the fairies were given their new wands to take a look at. They were lovely and shiny and shimmered like cut glass. Each one was engraved with their name. When Stinkerbell was given hers, she took it eagerly.

"Oh. It's beautiful, quite, quite beautiful," she cried, for she loved things that sparkled. Stinkerbell clutched the wand to her chest. It was already starting to lose its shimmer where her grubby little hands had been all over it, and when she was told to hand it back she steadfastly refused.

"But I love it," she said. "It's the most loveliest thing I've ever had. I've never had anything of my very own before, I don't *want* to give it back."

All the other fairies had handed in their wands to Miss Primslip, and they watched wide-eyed as Miss Primslip advanced towards Stinkerbell.

"Give me the wand back, Stinkerbell," she said firmly. "You've got to learn how to use it properly first. Wand lessons take place on Tuesdays and Thursdays – today's Monday. You can have it back tomorrow."

But Stinkerbell was having none of it. She held on to her wand with a grip of iron. Suddenly, Miss Primslip made a dash for it, and grabbing hold of the end of the wand, she began to pull.

"Let go!" seethed Miss Primslip through gritted teeth.

"Shan't," said Stinkerbell, tightening her grip.

"*Let go,*" screamed Miss Primslip, furious.

"Shan't!" said Stinkerbell, closing her eyes tight, determined to hold on to her treasured possession.

And then, just when it looked as if they would be locked in a tug-of-war until home-time, there was a sudden voluminous puff of smoke. It changed from pink to green, to purple and then back to pink again. And as it began to clear, a small shower of silver confetti appeared and sprinkled down on to the empty space where Miss Primslip had been standing just a moment ago.

The fairies gathered round and stared down at the little pile of silver bits. Meanwhile Stinkerbell, who up until now had kept her eyes firmly shut, cautiously opened one eye, and then the other. She chewed her bottom lip anxiously. "Oh dear. Oh deary, deary me."

Eventually the King was summoned, and he strode into the classroom just as all the dust had finally settled, leaving a thin, pink chalky film over the desks, the blackboard, and the worried faces of the young fairies.

"Where's Miss Primslip?" asked the King, frowning. The class was silent. Then, finally, Douglas put up his hand and said, "Please, your Majesty. I think she's exploded."

The King's eyes widened in astonishment. "Exploded! You say your teacher's *exploded*?"

"Yes, your Majesty," said Douglas, pointing towards the pile on the floor. "And I think you might be standing on her, as well."

The King looked horrified and quickly stepped off the little mound. He looked around at the shocked, dust-covered faces of the fairies.

"Now," he said crossly. "Which one of you blew up Miss Primslip? Come on. Own up."

There was silence. Finally, the King turned to a fairy who was standing next to him. "Hilary," he said firmly, "Go and get a dustpan and brush, and sweep up Miss Primslip. I'll see if I can get her back into one piece again."

The little fairy rushed off. Meanwhile, Stinkerbell, who was still holding her wand, put it carefully down on a nearby desk. Then with her hands clasped behind her, she began to back slowly out of the door.

The King's eyes fell upon her and they narrowed suspiciously. "Stinkerbell!" he said in a very low, deep voice. "Are *you* responsible for Miss Primslip's unfortunate predicament?"

Stinkerbell opened her mouth: "Well, your Majesty, yes, but—"

The King held up his hand and tut-tutted loudly. "For one week I have put up with your behaviour in my Kingdom. Now this has gone too far. I am banishing you from the garden."

"Oo! Where to, your Majesty? Abroad? Spain would be nice," said Stinkerbell sweetly.

"No, not Spain!" snapped the King. "Somewhere nearer than that – but far enough away to stop you doing any more damage. A place far more suitable for a fairy who – how shall I put it – a fairy who attracts dirt like a magnet. It's the *dustbin* for you, my girl!"

The King shook his head solemnly. "In all my years as King, I have never seen anything like it. Blowing up my barbecue palace was bad enough, but blowing up the teacher as well! Now, Stinkerbell, you can stay in the dustbin until you learn to behave yourself." And the King marched to the door and pointed his magnificent wand in the direction of the back gate. "Stinkerbell! You filthy fairy! GET IN THAT BIN!"

And off went young Stinkerbell shame-faced and with head bowed, across the lawn, past the sandpit, round the pond, until she reached the back gate.

She peered dubiously through the railings where the huge silver dustbin could be seen twinkling in the sunlight. It looked enormous, and extremely unwelcoming, like a tall monstrous tower. But Stinkerbell turned bravely round, and with a shake of her scruffy little plaits, announced in a very determined voice: "You might be banishing me to this Bustdin thing now – but you just wait. I'll be back!!"

CHAPTER
TWO

LIFE IN THE DUSTBIN was not as bad as Stinkerbell had imagined. In fact, it was pretty good. After all, rubbish was her hobby – and here it was delivered straight to her home! At least once a day, twice, if she was very lucky, someone would open the lid, and a cascade of all sorts of bits and pieces would be tipped all over her. It was bliss!

Stinkerbell found some good uses for the rubbish. She made herself some very nice furniture: a banana-skin hammock for a bed, a kipper-skin rug, and a yogurt-pot stool. She'd even made some curtains from the pages of a gardening magazine and pinned them to the side of the dustbin. Even though she didn't have a window, the pictures made her feel more at home.

However, Stinkerbell soon discovered a drawback of the dustbin: once a week, it was emptied. Fortunately, the first time it happened she wasn't in it. Unfortunately, all her furniture disappeared in an instant. But it was quite easy to collect it all over again – the people who lived in the house at Number 11 were very fond of bananas, kippers and yogurt.

One morning, Stinkerbell woke to a soft *tap, tap tapping* on top of her dustbin lid. This was followed by a jingling sound that seemed somehow familiar to her.

"Burglers!" declared Stinkerbell to herself. "I bet they're after my priceless jewel." And from under her teabag pillow she carefully pulled out a pink plastic tiara, no bigger than a thumbnail. Stinkerbell had found it inside a screwed-up paper bag the previous night. She thought it must be very valuable, and had

most probably belonged to a fairy princess.

"Well. This *nearly*, fairy princess has got it now," Stinkerbell said firmly, and plonked it down on top of her head between her scruffy plaits.

The tapping and jingling continued, and Stinkerbell, though still a little unsteady on her wings, flew up to investigate.

She heaved the lid of the dustbin off a fraction and peeped out. Standing on top of it, broom in hand, was Douglas. He looked extremely shifty, and was whistling nonchalantly to himself as he swept.

"Oh, it's you, Douglas," said Stinkerbell, looking disappointed. She'd rather it had been a burglar than him.

She looked at him suspiciously. "What are you doing here, anyway? You're not spying on me, are you?"

Douglas gave a little gulp, because that's *exactly* what he was doing. The King had told him to keep an eye on Stinkerbell, just to make sure she was behaving herself.

"Of course not," replied Douglas, sweeping harder. "I just thought I'd give your dustbin a bit of a clean while I had my broom out, that's all."

"Well, my dustbin doesn't need cleaning," replied Stinkerbell. She didn't believe a word. "I keep it very nice myself, thank you. Come and see."

Stinkerbell pushed the lid further back and sat on the edge with her feet dangling over the side. Douglas trotted over and peered in. The bin was half full and he'd never *seen* such a mess. And as for the smell – what a stink! The strongest aroma of all that came wafting up and into his nose was of bananas. Ripe, squashy bananas. Douglas stepped back, holding his nose.

"It's very nice, Stinkerbell," he said, pinching it tightly. "Very homely. Now, I really must be going, school starts in ten minutes and it's wand lessons first thing."

Stinkerbell watched him go, and as he hopped through the back gate and into the garden she gave a sigh. It wasn't fair. She was missing having proper flying lessons and, worst of all, wand lessons. She'd *never* get to have a proper wand at this rate.

Stinkerbell flew back into her bin despondently, and lay down on her hammock, staring up at the clouds floating by. Then suddenly they were blocked out as a huge hand loomed over and threw something into the bin. It was an old, mangled TV aerial.

Stinkerbell got up to take a look. Of course she had no idea what it really was, but she did know what it reminded her of. And with great excitement, she snapped off one of its antenna and polished it up with a piece of cotton wool. Next she inspected her filthy fingernails. Very carefully she managed to extract the tiny amount of fairy dust that had been wedged there ever since she blew up the barbecue.

Stinkerbell sprinkled it over the three prongs at the end of the antenna, and waited.

After a while she began to feel a slight tingling sensation. "It's working, it's working," she cried excitedly.

Quickly she flew outside and on to the grass below. Out on the street she could see a passer-by approaching. An old lady wearing a rather silly hat that looked like a giant pin-cushion.

Stinkerbell ran over to the pavement and waited for her to pass. Then she pointed the aerial and *PING!* half the old lady's big, daft hat disappeared.

Stinkerbell jumped up and down in her boots, hardly able to contain herself. She hadn't noticed that the wand was making some extremely strange noises, especially when the wind blew from the direction of the local TV station!

She knew that it wasn't the most beautiful wand she'd ever seen. But having a broken TV aerial was better than nothing at all. And anyway, thought Stinkerbell, holding it proudly out in front of her, from a distance, nobody could EVER tell the difference!

CHAPTER
THREE

LATER THAT AFTERNOON, Stinkerbell sat high up in an enormous oak tree. It was her favourite place because it overlooked the bottom of the garden. She adjusted herself on the edge of a branch, and peered through the leaves.

Over at the far side, all the fairies seemed to be out and about, flitting here and there, dusting the leaves and generally tidying up the flowerbeds.

"Humph!" snorted Stinkerbell, settling back against the branch and crossing her legs. "Look at them all. Racing around like a load of demented dragonflies. Busy, busy, busy. Work, work, work. That's all they *ever* seem to do." And she picked absent-mindedly at the hole in the knees of her tights, and admired her newly-acquired wand.

Now, if the truth be known, Stinkerbell was feeling rather lonely and left out. The only good thing about living in the dustbin was wallowing in the 24-hour trash. Apart from that, it was very dull, and much too quiet. She longed to have a chat with someone.

After a while, when she had almost decided to go home, Stinkerbell spotted Douglas. She could see him standing directly below holding his little watering can with DOUGLAS'S – DO NOT TOUCH painted very neatly on the side. She knew he was spying on her again because his can was empty, and he kept sneaking glances up into the tree.

"Psst. Douglas!" Stinkerbell hissed.

Douglas made out he couldn't hear her, and pretended to water a clump of forget-me-nots.

"Psst! Cloth-ears!" said Stinkerbell a little louder.

Douglas looked all around, squinting through his thick glasses, then he went on "watering".

Stinkerbell tutted loudly. "Stop ignoring me, Dougie," she said crossly. She pulled an acorn from a twig, and dropped it directly on to Douglas's head.

Douglas let out a cry and, rubbing the top of his woolly hat, he looked up.

"Who did that? Is that you, Stinkerbell?" he asked irritably.

"Of course it's me, you puny pixie. How many other fairies do you know who hang around in the tree-tops on a fine summer's afternoon? Is it safe to come down?"

Douglas looked around nervously. "No, it's not," he hissed. "And I'm not really supposed to talk to you. The King says you're a bad influence and reprobate, whatever that means."

"Well, it probably means that I'm good and kind and terribly beautiful, so I'm coming down anyway!" announced Stinkerbell. "Now just you wait there, and don't you move a miniscule muscle."

Douglas put down his watering can and nervously chewed his lip. He thought he'd better stay where he was. He was a bit scared of Stinkerbell, especially after the Miss Primslip escapade. Though luckily enough she had been put back together again, and after a few days' bed-rest, had recovered sufficiently to return to teaching.

Stinkerbell climbed half-way down the tree, clutching her wand, and flew the rest of the way. Landing next to Douglas, she could now see that the bottom of the garden was becoming extremely busy.

"What's going on?" she asked.

"We're holding a festival to celebrate the birth of the King and Queen's new baby," replied Douglas proudly, though he was eyeing Stinkerbell's curious wand with some trepidation.

"Wh-what's that?" he asked nervously.

Stinkerbell held out her wand. "Oh. Do you like it? It's my new wand. It works, well, sort of. Do you want to see?"

Douglas backed away, holding his little watering can tightly to his chest. "N-n-no. It's OK," he spluttered.

"I really must be getting back. The King has put me in charge of the catering – well, making the sandwiches, anyway."

Stinkerbell started jumping up and down in her hefty boots, making the little bell on Douglas's woolly hat ring.

"Oh can't you take me with you, Dougie dear?" she implored. "I just love a good do. Pleeasse!"

Douglas shook his head. "It's more than my job's worth," he replied. "Now, if you've quite finished, Stinkerbell, I'll be off." And he hurried away as fast as his little legs could carry him.

Stinkerbell put her hands on her hips and scowled. The last thing she wanted to do was miss the fairy festival. Somehow she just *had* to get back to the bottom of the garden.

After Douglas had gone, Stinkerbell thought of a plan. She ran quickly down to the garden seat where the two sentries were on duty. She hung on to one of the legs and swung from side to side as she surveyed the scene. She could see that the whole place was beginning to fill up and she recognised quite a few faces.

There were the fairies from next door, and the ones from across the road at Number 12. The pixies from the park were there, as well as the group who lived in the plant tubs in the foyer of the local bingo hall. She also noticed the elves from the adventure playground over the other side of the dual carriageway. The elves were a reckless bunch and Stinkerbell had hung around with them for a few days, but even for them she had proved too much of a handful.

Then Stinkerbell spotted the King. She spat on her hand, rubbed her face, and dried it on the sleeve of her jacket. Then she smoothed down her plaits and rubbed her boots on the backs of her tights. She still didn't look exactly presentable, but she called over to him anyway.

"Your Majesty. Cooee! Oh great one!" she shouted.

The King looked across, and with a frown, he marched over.

"Hmph, Stinkerbell," he said, "I might have guessed you'd show your grubby face around here. Douglas told me you were hanging about. I must say, that boy really does have the makings of a jolly fine pixie."

Stinkerbell grimaced, and thought what a little creep Douglas was, but she tried not to let it show. The King looked like he was in a good mood and now was her chance to soft-soap him.

"Um, your Majesty. Oh wonderful Majestic Master," said Stinkerbell sweetly. "I've weeded around the fish-pond, and I've even dusted The Great Grinning Ones this morning." (Though of course she hadn't.)

"I thought I told you to stay away from those two. They're highly dangerous," the King said sharply. "Mark my words, Stinkerbell. One day, when you least expect it, they'll gobble you up, and leave nothing but your boots behind."

"I know, your Majesty. But I also know how much you like the garden to look nice," said Stinkerbell, pulling a bright yellow duster from her jacket pocket and waving it wildly around. "So I took a risk and gave them a quick flick with this."

"Very admirable, I'm sure," said the King, "but you're still not coming in."

Stinkerbell's shoulders drooped, and she stuffed the duster back in her pocket. Then, glancing behind her, she saw that the King and Queen of Talbot Road, and their terribly spoilt daughter, Princess Lavinia, were heading towards them. Suddenly, and much to the King's astonishment, Stinkerbell let out the most enor-mous wail, lay down on the grass and began kicking her legs up and down and pummelling the ground with her fists. The King looked on with great embarrassment, as by now the Royal family had almost reached the garden seat.

"Get up, Stinkerbell!" he hissed. Then seeing the King and Queen frowning at him he gave them a smile.

"Cynthia! Reginald!" he cried. "How wonderful to see you again."

Stinkerbell wailed louder.

The Queen peered down at her. "Oh, the poor sweet dear little thing," she exclaimed, helping Stinkerbell to her feet. "She looks like she's been sleeping in a ditch. Honestly, Nigel, you don't treat your loyal subjects very well," she said sternly, as Stinkerbell wailed even louder and threw her arms dramatically around the Queen's neck.

"B-b-but you don't understand. This is Stinkerbell. She's not what she seems," protested the King.

"I know what she is, Nigel," replied the Queen of Talbot Road crossly. "She's a poor slip of a girl who wouldn't say boo to a goose! *That's* what she is!"

The King gulped in disbelief and Stinkerbell sniffed loudly.

"Would you like to come to the festival, dear?" the Queen asked Stinkerbell.

Stinkerbell nodded her head hard.

"Now, I think you should let her into the festival immediately, and we'll say no more about it," continued the Queen. "Follow me, my dear," and she patted the top of Stinkerbell's head lightly.

Stinkerbell followed obediently, keeping her head down and giving the occasional sniff for good measure. When she was safely past the bench she gave a little curtsey to the Queen.

"Oh thank you, your Majesty," she said sweetly. "You have made a poor orphaned fairy very happy."

"Not at all, my dear," replied the Queen. "Now run along and enjoy yourself."

When Stinkerbell was a safe distance from the King of her garden, she twirled around and around, then gave him a flamboyant wave with her wand. The King glared at her and shook his fist. Then he noticed the

Queen of Talbot Road eyeing him suspiciously, so he quickly turned it into a wave instead. Stinkerbell waved back and, blowing him a kiss, raced off. She was back at the bottom of the garden again and it felt *very, very* good.

CHAPTER
FOUR

THE FAIRY FESTIVAL was in full swing. All around the border of the garden were lots of tiny stalls selling everything from lucky pixie charms to fairy cakes.

Stinkerbell skipped around in her big clompy boots, looking at all the stalls with great interest. She was just inspecting a Green stall that was being run by two little leprechauns when she heard a loud sniff directly behind her. Stinkerbell turned around and saw Princess Lavinia, the King and Queen of Talbot Road's terribly spoilt and very pristine daughter. She was wearing a spotless white dress that stuck out like a lampshade, and she had four blond ringlets, two on either side of her head, that looked like big, fat sausages tied up with huge floppy bows. Her nose was stuck right up in the air, and she peered down it at Stinkerbell very distastefully and sniffed again.

"Your name's Stinkerbell, isn't it?" she asked in a snooty voice. "What a horrible name. My name's Lavinia, and *I'm* a Princess."

Stinkerbell looked at her crossly. "Stinkerbell is *not* a horrible name," she replied. "I love it. It's better than La-di-da Lavinia. What do people call you for short anyway – Lav? Sounds like lavatory to me!"

Princess Lavinia's eyes began to narrow, and she puckered up her lips.

"How dare you!" she seethed. "At least I'm not dirty. My mummy said you looked like you slept in a ditch."

Stinkerbell smoothed down her little potato-peeling skirt. "Well I don't, actually," she replied. "If you must know, I live in a dustbin."

Princess Lavinia's eyes widened, and she pulled a face. "In a dustbin? How disgusting!" she squealed. "No wonder you smell of squashy bananas!"

"What a cheek!" said Stinkerbell, hands on hips. "I do not smell of squashy bananas. I smell of old veg and damp newspaper and baked beans and kippers! And anyway, you don't look like a *real* princess. You haven't got a proper tiara to wear like me."

Princess Lavinia looked at Stinkerbell's tiny plastic crown. "Call that cheap old thing a tiara!" she giggled. "Let's face it, Stinkerbell, you look about as much like a fairy princess as – as – " Princess Lavinia pointed to a worm that was under one of the stalls – "As that disgusting, filthy thing!"

That was it. In an instant, Stinkerbell had picked up the worm, pulled up Princess Lavinia's dress and shoved it straight down the back of her frilly knickers!

"Serves you right," she said triumphantly. "And I hope it's all wet and slimy. You're lucky I didn't have a frog or a newt to hand, 'cause I'd have shoved *them* down your knicks as well!"

And with that she picked up her wand and stomped off, leaving Princess Lavinia writhing and squealing and jumping up and down, as she tried to extract the wriggling worm from her bright pink knickers.

Stinkerbell headed towards the other side of the garden. She had spotted something that looked very interesting. It was a tent made out of two handkerchiefs draped over a twig. Outside hung a sign that read: MYSTIC MABEL. FORTUNE TELLER TO THE STARS AND ROYALTY.

Mystic Mabel was an old tooth fairy (with no teeth, strangely enough. Stinkerbell often wondered why she didn't get a pair of dentures made up out of the ones she'd collected over the years!). She was renowned for her powers of prediction, so Stinkerbell thought she'd give her a try. She lifted up the corner of the handkerchief and stepped inside.

In the dark interior, old Mystic Mabel sat hunched over a table with a glass marble on it. This was her crystal ball. She peered through the gloom at Stinkerbell and, in a whistling, gummy sort of voice said, "Sit down and cross my palm with silver."

Stinkerbell plonked herself down on the chair opposite Mystic Mabel. "I'm afraid I don't have any silver," she announced loudly. "I'm flat broke. But I'd really like my fortune told, please, Mystic Mabel. And I don't want to hear anything boring or horrid. I want to hear that I'm going to get back to the bottom of the garden,

get my real wand and become a princess, and lots of lovely slushy things like that."

Mystic Mabel squinted at Stinkerbell through the darkness. "Stinkerbell! I thought I could smell you! Well, I suppose I'd better tell your fortune now you're here."

"Yes, please, Mab. Fire away."

Mystic Mabel stared deep into her crystal ball, which suddenly looked very dirty.

"Well? What can you see?" asked Stinkerbell.

"Er, hold on a minute," said Mystic Mabel. "It's looking a bit grubby."

She breathed hard on the ball, and rubbed it vigorously with the edge of her shawl. Then she stared intently into it again. The ball hadn't cleared very much, but she could just make out Stinkerbell's grubby little face, surrounded by empty boxes and screwed-up, greasy chip paper.

Stinkerbell leant forward eagerly. "Can you see me dressed in a diamond and ruby crown, sitting on a great big throne?" she asked excitedly.

"Um, well, no. Not exactly," replied Mystic Mabel hesitantly. "But I can see you sitting on *something*."

"Perhaps it's a small throne, next to the Queen's?" suggested Stinkerbell helpfully.

Mystic Mabel shook her head. "It doesn't look much like a throne," she said. "It isn't gold or chair-shaped. In fact it's sort of silver and round-looking."

Stinkerbell frowned. "What do you mean, silver and

round-looking? I've never seen a round silver throne. Perhaps it's a stool!" she added brightly. "I don't mind sitting on a silver stool."

Mystic Mabel shook her head again. "I'm afraid it doesn't look like that either. I'm sorry to say it looks very much like you're sitting on top of a dustbin."

"A DUSTBIN!" shouted Stinkerbell, jumping up. "You mean you saw my future and I was still in that flipping BIN! I don't believe a word. Give me that crystal ball, there must be some mistake."

"No, no. There's no mistake," Mystic Mabel insisted. "The ball never lies."

"Yes, it does," cried Stinkerbell. "It tells fibs and porkies, and it's told a great big whopper this time!"

And pulling the ball firmly out of the fortune-teller's grasp, she kicked it clean across the tent and smashed it into a supporting twig. Suddenly, the whole tent collapsed around their ears, and the next thing Stinkerbell knew the handkerchief was being lifted up, and the extremely cross face of the King was glaring down at her.

"Stinkerbell!" he roared. "I might have guessed that you'd be behind, not to mention *under*, all this."

Stinkerbell bit her bottom lip and stared imploringly at the King.

"I was just having my fortune told, your Majesty, and suddenly the tent caved in," replied Stinkerbell, not very convincingly. Then Mystic Mabel's head appeared from under the handkerchief as well. She looked very

cross and dishevelled, and one of her big hooped earrings was missing.

"She's broken my crystal ball, you know," she snapped. "Kicked it clean across the tent she did. Two hundred years old that ball was, and now that pesky fairy's gone and broken it!"

Stinkerbell looked indignant. "Well, no wonder it didn't tell my fortune properly, if it was *that* old," she scoffed. "You should buy a new one, you stingy old thing, you!"

"That's enough, Stinkerbell," said the King, grabbing her by her collar and pulling her out from beneath what had been the tent.

Stinkerbell dusted herself down, though it didn't

make much difference to her appearance. She straightened her tiara and picked her wand up proudly. Quite a crowd had gathered, including Douglas, who was blinking at her through his spectacles.

"I don't suppose we could forget this happened, could we?" asked Stinkerbell sweetly, clasping her hands behind her back and scraping the toes of her boots in the dirt.

The King shook his head. "Twenty minutes you've been back down the bottom of the garden. TWENTY MINUTES. And in that time you've scared the living daylights out of Princess Lavinia, pulled down Mystic Mabel's tent and smashed a priceless antique crystal ball."

"It was an accident," replied Stinkerbell with a shrug. "I slipped."

"It's just not good enough!" answered the King sternly. "You're a menace. And a *mess!* Fairies are supposed to be neat and tidy, and, well – *fairylike!* No, the bin is the best place for you, my girl." And once again he pointed towards the back gate.

"That's where you belong, Stinkerbell," he said firmly. "You're an insult to the fairy world, now – " and he said the words that made Stinkerbell shudder:

"GET BACK IN THAT BIN!!"

CHAPTER
FIVE

EVERYONE WATCHED as Stinkerbell made the long lonely journey back across the garden. When she reached The Great Grinning Ones, she stopped and looked back hopefully. The King shook his head and pointed his wand towards the back gate. Just as Stinkerbell was about to slip through the railings, she saw something out of the corner of her eye. By the back gate were some empty wine bottles. Stinkerbell peered through the green glass. She heard a giggle and then someone let out a big burp.

"Shh. Shh," a voice hissed from behind the bottles. Stinkerbell moved her head from side to side to try and make out the shapes through the glass. Then with dismay she realised who they were. Huddled behind the wine bottles were the most feared family in the neighbourhood. They were mean and nasty; they cheated and lied; and they stole things. They lived in a couple of beer crates inside an old deserted brewery. They were the Gobs, the horriblest creatures from the fairy world. All goblins were vicious and spiteful, but this family were meaner and nastier than any other goblins, and whenever their name was mentioned it sent shivers down a fairy's spine. All four of them wore long black jackets and pointed winklepicker shoes. Their jet-black hair was swept back into an enormous quiff with long sideburns. They had sharp rotten teeth and bad breath, and their fingernails were like birds' claws.

Stinkerbell tip-toed as best she could in her big boots around the side of the gate and peered carefully round the corner.

"'As she gone, Dad?" a little voice piped up. It was Dwayne Gob, the youngest son.

"Yeah, I think so. Though there's a funny smell lingering – bit like bananas," replied Mr Gob. Then he whispered: "Come on."

Stinkerbell pressed herself against the gate and watched as the whole family raced across the garden. Then quickly she flew up on to the brick wall, ran along it and then climbed up into the tree that she used for spying. Everyone below was quite unaware that the dreaded Gob family was about to descend on them, when suddenly there was the most terrible, scraping, squeaking noise. Everyone stopped what they were doing and looked towards the garden shed where Mr

Gob was slowly dragging his long fingernails down the windowpane.

"Ladies and gentleman," said Mr Gob, "Thanks for the invite. Though ours must have got lost in the post, 'cause me and the wife and our two little gobbys didn't get one."

The King stepped forward. "That's because we didn't send you one, Mr Gob," he said bravely. "You know you're not welcome here. We don't like thieves and bullies in our garden."

Mrs Gob pointed a finger at the King. "Oi. Watch who you're callin' a thief, you feeble fairy," she snapped. "I never stole nothing that wasn't worth stealin'." And she let out a shrill piercing shriek of laughter that made everyone cover their ears.

"That's right," agreed Mr Gob. "And this time we've come for just one thing. A new recruit. A fresh young elf or pixie, or even a fairy would do." Mr Gob looked around at everyone. The young fairies were quaking. They'd heard terrible stories about the Gob family, about how they kept fairies prisoner and fed them nothing but pickled onions. And then they sent them out to pick pockets and shoplift, and if they failed to return with anything they were hung upside-down for three days, or made to stand on one leg for hours on end. Nobody wanted to join the Goblin Gang, no *fear*, no thank you very *much*!

Stinkerbell watched intently through the leaves as the Gob family scanned the crowd, looking for a suitable victim. Suddenly Elvis, the oldest Gob son, pointed excitedly.

"I seen one, Dad. I seen one," he cried, jumping up and down.

"Which one, son?" asked Mr Gob, licking his lips, his eyes narrowing and twinkling with excitement.

"'Im over there in the thick specs and the daft hat with the bell on the end," replied Elvis Gob, pointing straight at Douglas. Douglas's face dropped and he blinked rapidly through his glasses.

"I've 'eard stories about what a goody two-shoes you are," said Elvis Gob, sneering at him. "What do you want to be helpful for? Why don't you come and join us and learn to be 'orrible?"

Douglas shook his head and backed nervously away. "Oh n-n-ooo," he stammered. "I couldn't possibly. I'm at Charm School, you see, and I'm working my way up to be in charge of the compost heap."

The two Gob brothers shrieked with laughter.

"Blimey, mate," said Elvis Gob sarcastically, "you pixies really do live life in the fast lane, don't yer?" And he whipped a comb out of his back pocket and ran it through his enormous quiff. Then Mr Gob butted in.

"Right. We've got no time to hang about talking to the likes of you. Are you going to come quietly, pixie boy, or will me and the missus have to use other means?"

"Don't you dare," interrupted the King.

"Oh shut up," sneered Mrs Gob, and waving her long skinny hands above her head she began to chant:

"Claw of crow. Eye of newt.
Once again the Gobs recruit.
Who shall we pick? It's hard to tell.
But we'll take the one with the specs and bell."

And she thrust her finger straight at Douglas. Immediately she did, all the other fairies stood on one leg and became rooted to the spot.

"It's no use, Douglas," cried the King. "She's gone and put the dastardly and illegal 'wobbling on one leg' spell on us. We won't be able to move for hours." He glared at Mrs Gob. "I hope you realise that this spell is

59

banned in every country in the world *except New Zealand*. You'd better make a run for it, Douglas."

But Douglas, who was a little slow on the uptake, did not move quickly enough, because the next thing he knew, the Gob brothers had tied his hands behind his back and were dragging him away. In the scuffle Douglas's glasses fell off and the sharp toe of Dwayne Gob's winklepicker stepped on the lens and cracked it.

"My glasses!" cried poor old Douglas. And Elvis Gob picked them up and shoved them crookedly on the end of Douglas's nose as he stumbled along between them.

Meanwhile, Mr and Mrs Gob were running amuck with a large sack, stuffing it with all sorts of valuables, like the Queen of Talbot's tiara, and the King of Ruskin Drive's big gold medallions. Then, just as they were about to leave, Mrs Gob spotted something lying in the centre of a flower. Kicking its legs contentedly in the air, and without a care in the world, was the King and Queen's brand-new baby.

"Ooo, look!" cried Mrs Gob, clapping her bony hands together. "It's a baby. We'll 'ave that away, it might come in handy."

And to the gasps of the King and Queen and all the other fairies, she scurried over, scooped up the baby and dropped it inside the sack! Then, within a matter of seconds, the Gob family, Douglas and the Royal fairy baby were gone.

Stinkerbell, who had of course seen everything, shouted down from the tree. "Don't you worry, your

Majesty. I'll get your baby back."

"Oh please!" cried the Queen, wobbling on one leg.

"And don't forget Douglas," added the King, who was having great difficulty keeping his balance. Stinkerbell pulled a face.

"Oh yes, him," she replied, wrinkling her nose up. "Can't he stay where he is? I'm sure he'll be much happier living with the Gobs."

"Stinkerbell!" roared the King, shaking his fist. "For once in your life just do as you're told! Unfortunately, you're our only hope as this spell won't wear off for hours. So GET GOING!"

"OK, OK, keep your hair on," replied Stinkerbell, holding her hands up. "Trust me. I'll get your baby *and* dreary Douglas back, if I must."

And with that she flew down and with grim determination pounded across the lawn clutching her TV aerial wand tightly in her fist. She wasn't at all sure how she was going to get them back, but one thing was certain, if she pulled this off, the King would be pleased and she'd *surely* get back down to the bottom of the garden.

Stinkerbell gave a little skip and a jump. Yes. This was definitely her big chance to come up smelling of roses instead of rotten old rubbish!

CHAPTER
SIX

STINKERBELL SET OFF in hot pursuit up the road. Though she had never actually been there before, she did know that the Gobs lived inside the old brewery past a row of shops, a small park and round the corner from the Post Office. At last, having nearly been stepped on by someone coming out of the greengrocer's, weed on by a dog, and almost pulverised by a pushchair, Stinkerbell turned the corner and saw the large, imposing, derelict building looming over her. It looked just like the sort of place that the Gobs would hang out in.

Stinkerbell clutched her wand tighter and saw ahead a huge rusty iron door which was open just wide enough to squeeze through. Inside, it was vast. Stinkerbell had never been in anything so big before. There were long, thin windows that went all the way up to the ceiling. Most of them were smashed – it was very draughty. Over in the far corner, Stinkerbell could see the Gob family huddled round a little twig fire. They were arguing about something and sharing a bottle of Goblin Guck, a potent mixture that goblins all over the world are notorious for drinking.

Stinkerbell tip-toed a little closer. Suddenly Mr Gob

swung round on his beer crate. "Who's there?" he demanded.

"It's me, Mr Gob, Stinkerbell from Azalea Avenue," said Stinkerbell in a friendly voice.

Mr Gob's eyes narrowed. "Aren't you that weird filthy fairy who lives in a bin or somethin'? What are you doin' in this neck of the woods, girl?"

Dwayne Gob bounced up and down frantically on his beer crate. "Jumping blue suede shoes, Dad. It *is* her!" he cried, dribbling with excitement.

"Shut up," snapped his father and stuck his pointy chin out. "What do you want? I hope you 'aven't come for yer mate. 'Cause we 'ain't givin' 'im up. Nor the baby, neither."

"Oh no, Mr Gob," replied Stinkerbell sweetly. "I want to join your gang. I'm sick and tired of living in that dustbin and being treated like a second-class fairy. I want to learn to steal and cheat and lie, just like you lot do."

Mr Gob smiled, showing all his rotten old pointy teeth. "Good for you, girl. Good for you. We always welcome new recruits. 'Ere, 'ave a swig of Goblin Guck. It'll put hairs on yer chest. Not to mention the soles of yer feet!" he said, and handed Stinkerbell a dusty-looking dark brown bottle. She only pretended to take a sip, as she really didn't fancy having hair on her chest or her feet! And besides that, it smelt absolutely disgusting, far worse than anything that had ever been thrown into her dustbin.

Mrs Gob looked her up and down. "You don't look much like a fairy, do you?" she remarked, sniffing loudly and wiping her pointy nose on her sleeve. "I mean, all the fairies I've ever seen are a right snooty-looking bunch. And as for that pixie we brought in. What's 'is name? Douglas? He's a right namby-pamby. He 'asn't stopped blubbing since we got 'ere. Mr Gob's threatened 'im with everything, from unravelling 'is woolly hat and 'anging 'im upside-down by the thread, to flushing 'im down the toilet. Talk about a cry baby. And when we've been so reasonable an' offered 'im a bright new career hopportunity!"

"Well, I'm not like that," said Stinkerbell, adamantly. "Though I am a fairy; I just happen to be special, that's all." She looked at each of the Gobs in turn. Never had she seen such a disgusting family. But Stinkerbell knew she had to convince them that she wanted to become a goblin, so she could rescue Douglas and the King and Queen's baby. So far she seemed to be doing OK. The Gobs seemed to believe her. But then again, they weren't blessed with many brains between them.

"Right then. Where do I start?" demanded Stinkerbell, clapping her hands determinedly together.

"Well, first you got to give yer wand up," said Elvis Gob. "Goblins don't 'ave wands. We're too tuff, see."

"Fine, fine," replied Stinkerbell, a little uneasy. She hadn't counted on handing her wand over. Useless as it was, she always felt a little lost without it. However, she gave it to Elvis Gob, who snatched it away.

"It looks like a telly aerial," he said, inspecting it closely.

"It is. I made it into a wand myself," said Stinkerbell proudly.

Elvis Gob stared at Stinkerbell and then down at the wand. Then he stared back up at Stinkerbell and then back down at the wand again. Then he finally asked: "Does it get Satellite telly?" He really was stupid!

"Right then. I'll take you to yer mate," said Mr Gob, polishing off the dregs of Goblin Guck and giving a loud belch.

"Oh, Douglas isn't my friend," replied Stinkerbell. "He's always telling tales on me."

"Still, maybe you can make him see some sense," said Mr Gob, putting a long skinny arm around Stinkerbell's shoulders. "You know, the life of a goblin is great. You get to be feared and loathed and hated. You never get asked to go places. Other fairies would rather walk over hot coals than spend an evening with you. And no one, ever, *ever*, returns your calls. It's brilliant!"

"Sounds t'riffic," replied Stinkerbell, thinking that life in the dustbin was like one long party compared to this!

CHAPTER
SEVEN

MR GOB AND HIS TWO SONS led Stinkerbell to Douglas.
He was sitting on a rickety old chair, and blubbing into
his handkerchief. When he saw Stinkerbell he gasped.
"What are you doing here, Stinkerbell? Have you

been captured as well? Isn't it ghastly. I don't want to be a goblin. I'll have to be mean and nasty and have a quiff. I don't want to be mean and nasty and have a quiff! I just want to go home!" And he bawled even louder into his already sodden handkerchief.

"Oh for goodness sake stop it, Douglas," snapped Stinkerbell, "and just do as they say."

Douglas, who was used to doing as he was told, sniffed loudly and sat up on his chair.

"So where do we start then, Mr Gob?" said Stinkerbell, her hands on her hips. "I can't wait to learn the tricks of your trade."

"Well, I think we'll teach you the fine art of picking pockets first," replied Mr Gob. His long bony finger and thumb plucked an imaginary object from thin air.

"Ooo – is that like needlework?" asked Douglas, perking up a bit. "I'm good at sewing."

"No, it *isn't*. It's like thieving," snapped Elvis Gob, snatching Douglas's hankie and stuffing it into his back pocket, leaving just a small corner poking out. Then Dwayne Gob very nonchalantly strolled across the floor, and as he passed his brother, as quick as a flash, he whipped the handkerchief out of his pocket and ran off with it.

"Gosh. That's impressive," said Stinkerbell, trying to stifle a yawn.

"Is Dwayne going to give it back now?" asked Douglas, squinting through his broken glasses.

"Don't be daft, boy," said Mr Gob. "He nicked it. Now it's his."

"But it's *mine*," insisted Douglas. "My Aunty Beverley bought it for me last Christmas. It's one of a matching set."

Dwayne and Elvis looked like they were going to do something rather unpleasant to Douglas at any moment, so Stinkerbell stepped in.

"Oh this is great," she said enthusiastically. "What other illegal things can you teach us to do, Mr Gob?"

Mr Gob continued to show them how to cheat at everything from Poker to Pontoon. And at every board game from Ludo to Cluedo, from Mousetrap to Monopoly. And finally from Dominoes to Darts.

He then proceeded to tell lies so big that they could have filled the whole of the room they were standing in. But worst of all, much worse, he and his two stoogy sons showed them how to steal anything and everything from a two-pence piece to a tin of rice pudding. Stinkerbell, unfortunately, was quite good at all these things, though she had never stolen anything because she knew it was wrong. (She insisted that she was only *borrowing* the Action Man boots!) She had certainly told a few tiny white lies.

Douglas on the other hand was useless. Every time he pinched something he gave it back. Each time he told a lie, he'd say it wasn't true. And he simply could not cheat at board games.

The afternoon wore on and soon it grew dark. Stinkerbell still hadn't worked out just how she was going to escape with Douglas and the baby. But after Mrs Gob had given them each a pickled onion sandwich for their supper, and she had watched Mr Gob eat five great doorstep slabs, all washed down with the foul smelling Goblin Guck, Stinkerbell had an idea.

"Um, Mr Gob," she said slowly, putting down her sandwich. "I know a game that we haven't played yet, that you can REALLY cheat at."

Mr Gob eyed her suspiciously, one bushy eyebrow cocked. "What's that, then?" he asked, chomping on his enormous crunchy sandwich. "I thought we'd 'bout covered the cheating at games side of things," he mumbled, spitting out bits of onion all over the place as he spoke.

Stinkerbell shook her head. "Not quite, Mr Gob. You've left out Hide-and-Seek. It's possible to *really* cheat at that."

"Oh yeah," sneered Elvis Gob, running a comb through his greasy hair. "How's that, then?"

"Well," said Stinkerbell, sitting up on her seat eagerly. "When it's your turn to hide, you hide so well that no one can possibly *ever* find you."

Mr Gob stroked his pointy chin thoughtfully. "Yeah, I 'adn't thought of that one before," he said. "Let's give it a go. I reckon I know somewhere where you'll NEVER find us Gobs."

"OK. Douglas and I will close our eyes and count to a hundred," said Stinkerbell. "And you lot go and see if you can hide so well that even we can't find you."

The Gobs could hardly contain themselves, and they went hurrying off to hide, arguing as they went.

"And remember," shouted Mr Gob from the other side of the vast room, "no peeking!"

"Don't worry, we won't," called Stinkerbell. "But just remember to hide well."

And she watched them disappear through a half-open door and out to the back of the brewery. As soon as they'd gone, Douglas closed his eyes and started counting. Stinkerbell looked at him as though he were quite mad and when he got to thirty-six, she thumped him.

"What are you doing, Douglas, you daft pixie?!" she said.

"I'm counting to a hundred, of course," replied Douglas. "I thought we were playing Hide-and-Seek."

"We're going to *escape*, Douglas," replied Stinkerbell. "Just give those gormless Gobs enough time to hide so that even *they* won't know where they've hidden, and then we'll be off."

Douglas looked disappointed. "Oh, we're not going to go and find them then?" he asked. "I rather like playing Hide-and-Seek. But not as much as I like playing 'I Spy'."

Stinkerbell shook her head. "You're so stupid sometimes, Dougie dear, that I think you and the compost heap deserve each other. Come on." And she quickly picked up her wand. Then she looked inside the sack, which the Gobs had hung up on a nail, and, checking that the King and Queen's baby was still there, she hoisted the sack over her shoulder and led the way out of the brewery into the cold night air.

CHAPTER
EIGHT

DOUGLAS HAD NEVER been outside in the dark before and he clung tightly on to the back of Stinkerbell's jacket as they made their way through the tall coarse grass and on to the pavement. Once there, they could see a little better, as the road ahead was bathed in the orange glow of the street lamps.

"Why's everything orange?" whispered Douglas, fearful that the Gobs might hear him. "Is this the colour of night-time?"

Stinkerbell shook her head and explained that street lights were for people who wanted to walk about at night.

"What do they want to go and do that for?" replied Douglas. "You wouldn't catch me out in the dark, no fear. I'd rather be tucked up in bed under my nice warm duvet, thank you very much."

"Well, come on then," said Stinkerbell, walking off in the direction of the Post Office. "Otherwise the Gobs will realise we're not coming after them, and then we'll have to go back to a life of pickled onion sandwiches and dreary board games."

Douglas ran quickly after her and they set off towards Azalea Avenue. As they turned the corner by the Post Office and went past the row of shops, Stinkerbell just managed to save Douglas from falling down a newly-dug hole in the pavement.

"Who put that thing there?" asked Douglas indignantly. "You don't think it's a trap the Gobs have set up for us, do you? Maybe they're waiting to catch us at the bottom," he added fearfully, and peered nervously down into it.

"No, I don't think so, Douglas," scoffed Stinkerbell. "The Gobs are probably still hiding somewhere, but sooner or later even that bunch of half-wits will wonder where we've got to. Come on."

And off they set once more. Stinkerbell thought she might be able to fly a short way, but what with having to carry the sack, as well as having Douglas holding on to her, it was virtually impossible to get off the ground. She found flying over great distances quite hard anyway as she'd been absent for all of the flying lessons at Charm School, because she'd been banished to that darn dustbin! It was also no good asking Douglas, because a pixie will avoid flying at all costs. They just don't like it, something to do with a fear of heights combined with air sickness. Stinkerbell thought it was typical of Douglas's mob to be like this. Pixies just had no sense of adventure.

Finally, Stinkerbell could see the familiar street lights and trees of Azalea Avenue. The dawn was breaking and the sky was a beautiful shade of orangey-red.

Suddenly, Douglas let out a little scream and clapped a hand over his mouth. "W-what's t-that thing?" he stammered, his eyes wide.

"What thing where?" tutted Stinkerbell crossly,

looking around. She was becoming distinctly tired of Douglas's company and she wanted to be rid of him as soon as possible.

Douglas pointed a shaky finger. "That monster thing

over there, with one leg and three flashing heads," said Douglas. "Look! Look at it. It's enormous. Come on, Stinkerbell, quickly, before it sees us."

Stinkerbell caught the waist of Douglas's trousers and pulled him back. "It's a traffic light, you pudding-brained pixie!" she said. "It can't hurt you. Honestly, Douglas, don't you know anything?!"

"No, I don't," replied Douglas haughtily. "And I don't ever want to set foot out of the garden again. The world outside is too dangerous for me."

At last Stinkerbell saw that they had reached the wall at the back of the house.

"Oh, thank goodness we're home," said Douglas. He breathed a sigh of relief and mopped his brow with the other hankie from his matching set. Stinkerbell flew up on to her dustbin lid, put the sack down and then helped Douglas up.

As they rested for a few minutes, they heard the familiar *click, click, click* of the Gobs's winklepicker shoes running along the pavement.

"You cheats! You tricked us!" cried Elvis, running up to the dustbin and shaking his fist at Stinkerbell.

"Hours we was hiding," said Mr Gob. "Hours stuck inside an empty Coke can. And let me tell you, it was no joke. My wife hasn't brushed her teeth for three years. And the last time my sons changed their socks and underpants was Christmas 1988 when my wife knitted them some new ones! They smell worse than you do, Stinkerbell!"

Dwayne Gob scratched the back of his trousers. "Yeah, and flippin' itchy these woolly pants are too!" he mumbled sulkily to himself.

"Well, Yah Boo Sucks!" called out Stinkerbell, dancing on top of her dustbin lid. "I'm not afraid of you lot. I may be a bit on the pongy side, but at least I don't cheat and steal, and I *never* tell lies."

Douglas looked at her in amazement. Stinkerbell gave him a sidelong glance. "Well, not often," she added truthfully with a shrug. "Anyway, if you take one step nearer, I'll use my wand on you and I shan't be responsible for its actions. The stories about its irregular behaviour are all true, you know," she added, thrusting the TV aerial in the Gobs's general direction. They backed off.

"Eeeh. We didn't want the stupid pixie, anyway," replied Mr Gob from a safe distance. "There's plenty more where he came from. I've heard there's a whole load of fairies just moved into the loading bay at the back of that new supermarket in the High Street. I think me and the missus will go and recruit one of them instead."

Dwayne and Elvis, who had been standing there picking their long pointy noses for about five minutes, looked up at Stinkerbell.

"Just you watch out, Stinkerbell," said Elvis. "Me and my brother won't forget that you escaped from us. We'll be looking for you."

Stinkerbell pulled herself up to her full height. "Oh,

I'm quaking in my boots, boys," she said sarcastically, knocking her knees together and pretending to tremble. Though really she was very glad to be back on her own territory. That Gob family really were a horrible bunch.

Just as the Gobs turned to leave, Douglas, who had been sitting quietly next to Stinkerbell on the dustbin lid, coughed lightly.

"Er, excuse me," he said politely. Mr Gob turned and looked at him crossly.

"What do you want?" he snapped. "I hope you realise that thanks to your fairy mate there you got off very lightly."

"Oh, I do. I do," insisted Douglas.

"Well, what is it then?" said Mrs Gob, putting her bony hands on her bony hips.

"Well, I was just wondering whether I could have my hankie back now?" asked Douglas, blinking innocently behind his spectacles.

Before the Gobs could answer, Stinkerbell grabbed hold of Douglas's arm, hoisted him off the dustbin lid, and quickly marched him back down to the bottom of the garden. There they found the King and all the other fairies still standing on one leg, rooted to the spot.

CHAPTER
NINE

"AH, THERE YOU ARE, Stinkerbell," said the King. "You took your time, didn't you? All night we've been standing here, it was most unpleasant, and I've got terrible pins and needles," he complained ungratefully.

"Oh, pardon me," replied Stinkerbell with a sniff. "But that was a very dangerous mission that you sent me on, and it's not my fault if the Gobs's 'Standing on One Leg' spell hasn't worn off yet. Anyway, here's Douglas back safe and sound for you." And she pushed Douglas in front of her.

"Splendid," replied the King. "We didn't want to lose a hard-working pixie like Douglas to such a lazy good-for-nothing bunch." He looked at Stinkerbell with one eyebrow raised inquisitively. "I don't suppose *you* thought of staying over that side of the neighbourhood, did you, Stinkerbell?" he added hopefully.

Stinkerbell looked most put out. "No I did not, your Majesty," she snapped. "In fact, I was rather hoping that you might give me another chance at the bottom of the garden. I'd pull my weight, and do the chores, and wash and *never* play tricks and—"

The King held his hand up. "That's enough," he announced. "I shall have to think about this,

Stinkerbell. Now, the Queen and I are most anxious to see our baby. Could you hand him over, please."

Stinkerbell looked blankly at him. "The baby please, Stinkerbell," repeated the King slowly.

Stinkerbell's face began to drop, and then she put her little hand to her mouth. "Oh, dear," she said, "I'm afraid I put him in the dustbin for safe-keeping."

The King tried to move, but he was still stuck fast. Then he checked his watch.

"Do you know what time it is, Stinkerbell?" he said, taking a deep breath.

Stinkerbell shook her head and bit her lip.

"It's half past eight," cried the King. "And do you by any chance know what day it is?"

Stinkerbell shook her head again and chewed her lip a little harder.

"It's Wednesday," announced the King. "And do you know what happens at half past eight on a Wednesday morning, Stinkerbell?"

This time Stinkerbell nodded her head as in the distance the low rumblings of an enormous truck could be heard, and all together the King, Queen, Douglas and Stinkerbell shouted in horror:

"THE DUSTBIN MEN ARRIVE!!"

"Oh dear," said Stinkerbell. "I'm ever so sorry, I just forgot."

"Forgot!" roared the King, trying to jump up and down on one leg. "You forgot! You threw the heir to the throne in the dustbin and then you 'just forgot' him! Go and retrieve him immediately and I just hope for your sake that you're not too late, you irresponsible fairy!"

Once again Stinkerbell half ran and half flew across the vast lawn, and around to the back gate. She was just in time to see the dustmen throw the contents of her dustbin into the back of the cart.

"Oh dear," said Stinkerbell again. "Oh deary, deary me."

And quick as a flash she flew up on to the tailgate of the huge lorry. Down below she could see all the rubbish being churned up and swallowed. Stinkerbell looked frantically for the tiny sack amongst all the drinks cartons, cans, carrier bags and boxes. It was worse than looking for a needle in a haystack. Then, to her relief, she suddenly spotted it. Somehow it had got caught on the corner of the grinder. It was swinging dangerously backwards and forwards, and from side to side. It looked as if it might fall off at any moment. Stinkerbell was some distance from it. She tried leaning over to grab hold of it, but she couldn't quite reach. The drop below into the grinder was very steep: it was like standing on the very edge of a cliff.

Suddenly the truck started to pull away and Stinkerbell almost lost her balance. For a second or two she wobbled backwards and forwards precariously on top of the tailgate. The little sack also swung backwards and forwards harder. Stinkerbell regained her balance and gripped her wand tightly. She felt like she was on a tightrope. The last time she had done this sort of thing was when she had been showing off by balancing on the washing line in the back garden. That hadn't ended very well either, because she'd fallen off and landed face-down in a puddle, taking half the washing on the line with her. The last thing she wanted to do was to fall off into this contraption.

Very carefully she edged her way along. Each time the truck stopped and started, she tried hard to keep her balance, and every time it did stop, another pile of rubbish would go hurtling over the top of her head, missing her by inches. She got clipped around the ear by an empty milk carton; had vanilla ice-cream trickling down her back and, to top it all, a half-eaten fried egg smacked her in the face. But Stinkerbell, who was made of stern stuff, managed to hold on. She thought about doing a spell to get the sack to come to her, but she knew she couldn't take the chance. Her wand was so unreliable it was likely to send the sack and the brand-new baby hurtling into the very depths of the dustcart.

Just as she thought she couldn't get any filthier or hang on any longer, the cart swerved, and Stinkerbell managed to scoop the sack up on the end of her wand. She pulled it towards her and clutched the bundle to her chest. As soon as the truck stopped again Stinkerbell flew down to the pavement and, dodging the big-booted feet of the dustbin men, ran up the road.

She was covered in dust and dirt from head to foot, she had bits of goodness-knows-what in her hair, there was ice-cream all down her back and one of the points of her tiara had snapped off. But she had the King's brand-new baby again.

She leapt over the wall into the front garden of 11 Azalea Avenue and nipped nimbly through the wrought iron bars of the gate to the back garden. She clutched the little sack to her chest, determined not to lose it this time. She ran across the lawn, and then, just as she reached the fish pond, she saw the two unmistakable figures of Dwayne and Elvis Gob. She tried to run past them, but Dwayne's long winklepicker shoe shot out and tripped poor Stinkerbell up so she landed flat on her face and dropped the sack.

"Gotcha!" cried Elvis triumphantly. "A Gob never forgets."

And he picked up the sack and threw it to his brother.

"Ha ha!" cried Dwayne, shaking the sack at Stinkerbell. "We win!"

Stinkerbell watched despondently as the long skinny figures of Dwayne and Elvis retreated up the garden chucking the sack to each other as they went. She felt

powerless to do anything against both of them. It looked like she'd lost the King and Queen's baby for good this time, and her chances of getting back down to the bottom of the garden were dashed forever.

CHAPTER
TEN

STINKERBELL PICKED HERSELF UP and sat dejectedly down on the edge of the pond. She was tired and hungry. Then, all of a sudden, an idea started to form. She turned slowly around and looked up. Staring down at her were the large, shiny red faces of The Great Grinning Ones. Stinkerbell leapt up, and quickly ran behind The Great Grinning One who was holding the fishing rod. Grabbing a leaf from a nearby bush, she rolled it up into a cone shape, then taking a deep

breath she held it up to her mouth like a megaphone and shouted through it. It was surprisingly loud.

"Oi! You two with the pointy shoes and ridiculous haircuts. Stop at once!" cried Stinkerbell from behind the garden gnome.

Elvis and Dwayne swung round, their mouths agape.

"Great Balls of Fire, Elv, what was that?" Dwayne said, dribbling nervously down the front of his jacket.

"It's me, The Great Grinning One!" shouted Stinkerbell.

Elvis and Dwayne clung to each other.

"It's that monstrosity over there," said Elvis, chewing the end of his bootlace tie frantically. "It's alive!"

From behind the gnome, Stinkerbell was trying hard not to laugh. She coughed a few times and continued. "If you don't put that sack down right now I shall come after you, attach you both to the end of my rod and use you as bait. Now, what's it to be, the baby or the bait?!"

"The baby, the baby!" cried Dwayne, putting the sack down and putting his hands up. "Take it. We don't want it. My mum told us to come back for it, but she only wanted someone small enough to fit inside the slot of the chocolate machine by the bus shelter."

"Right then," boomed Stinkerbell. "Don't let me see your horrible faces around here again. Otherwise you'll both be dangling on the end of this hook for the rest of your teenage years. Now, be off with you."

And as quick as greased lightening and twice as slippery, the two Gob brothers raced off.

By now, the spell on the other fairies had finally worn off and everyone gathered around Stinkerbell to congratulate her on the bravery of her clever plan to scare Dwayne and Elvis into a hasty retreat.

"Oh, it was nothing," said Stinkerbell modestly. "Those Gobs don't worry me. They're as stupid as the day is long. I knew I could fool them."

"That's as may be, Stinkerbell," replied the King, who had at last managed to retrieve his baby from the sack – and all the jewels the Gobs had stolen. The baby did not appear to be any the worse for wear after its ordeal, though it was looking a rather sickly green colour from having been swung around so much.

"You showed great initiative," said the King proudly.

"Thanks very much," said Stinkerbell. Though she wasn't sure whether showing initiative was a good or bad thing. Douglas, who was standing behind the King, looked green with envy, anyway.

"Maybe I underestimated you," continued the King. "So I am willing to let bygones be bygones and give you another chance at the bottom of the garden."

All the other fairies gave a little cheer, though it was a bit half-hearted because none of them were quite sure they really wanted Stinkerbell living with them again. They liked her, but she did make life just a bit too hair-raising.

"Oh thank you, your Majesty," gasped Stinkerbell, throwing her arms around the King and giving him a great big sloppy and very grubby kiss bang on the lips!

"Now, now, don't get carried away," said the King, disentangling himself. "I'll start you off on a few simple tasks, and I think I'll leave Douglas in charge of you."

Stinkerbell wrinkled her nose up at Douglas behind the King's back. Douglas looked extremely apprehensive.

"Do you think you can handle this?" asked the King seriously, putting a hand on Douglas's shoulder. "This could lead you one step nearer to the compost heap, you know."

At the very mention of the compost heap, Douglas's eyes began to twinkle. He saw himself standing on top of it, and seeing for miles around all the other gardens

in the street, or marching up and down in front of it
making sure that it was kept in a nice tidy pile.

"What a job!" thought Douglas dreamily to himself.
"What a job!"

He snapped back to earth with a bump. "Oh, I'm
sure Stinkerbell and I will get on just fine, your
Majesty," said Douglas, telling his very first white lie.

Meanwhile, Stinkerbell had dashed back to her

dustbin to retrieve her only two possessions: a tooth-brush and a rather faded snapshot of her parents, the size of a postage stamp. These were stuck to the base of the dustbin lid with a piece of bubblegum, to make sure they never mistakenly got thrown away.

Perhaps I should have done that with the King and Queen's baby, thought Stinkerbell to herself as she skipped merrily back. Oh well, it didn't matter now. Because she was finally back down at the bottom of the garden. And she'd NEVER have to hear those dreaded words: "GET BACK IN THAT BIN," again!

The King, on the other hand, wasn't so sure. He was already having second thoughts as he watched young Stinkerbell come skipping towards him in her big, hefty boots, her filthy face beaming, a fly buzzing around the top of her head.

He also noticed that she seemed to be leaving a long sticky trail of what could only be vanilla ice-cream behind her. It ran all the way from the gate to the heel of her boot. Most peculiar!

"Oh well," sighed the King. "Perhaps *this* time she'll change."

And as Stinkerbell passed the seat and stepped once more into the bottom of the garden, he thought maybe, just maybe, he was right ...

What do YOU think?